KORA AND KA

H. D.

KORA AND KA
WITH MIRA-MARE

INTRODUCTION BY ROBERT SPOO

A NEW DIRECTIONS

Bibelot

Manufactured in the United States of America.
New Directions Books are printed on acid-free paper.
Published simultaneously in Canada by Penguin Books Canada
Limited.

This edition was first printed privately in 1934 for the author's friends
by Imprimerie Darantiere at Dijon, France. An original copy was gra-
ciously provided by H.D.'s daughter, Perdita Schaffner.
First published as a New Directions Bibelot in 1996.

"Mira-Mare" appears on page 57.

Library of Congress Cataloging-in-Publication Data

H. D. (Hilda Doolittle), 1886-1961.
    Kora and Ka / H. D. ; introduction by Robert Spoo.
       p.   cm.
    "Originally printed privately in 1934 for the author's friends by
    Imprimerie Darantiere at Dijon, France—T.p. verso.
    Contents: Kora and Ka — Mira-Mare.
    ISBN 0-8112-1317-X (acid-free paper)
    1. Manners and customs—Fiction.   I. H. D. (Hilda
    Doolittle), 1886-1961.   Mira-Mare   II. Title
    PS3557.0726K6   1996
    811'.52—dc20   96-1426
                                CIP

Celebrating 60 years of publishing for James Laughlin
by New Directions Publishing Corporation,
80 Eighth Avenue, New York 10011

As she took care to note on their title pages, H.D. wrote "Kora and Ka" and "Mira-Mare" in the Swiss canton of Vaud in 1930. She liked to think of them as "long-short stories," a usefully elastic genre in a period when writer's block and personal worries often conspired to paralyze her art. H.D. approached the craft of fiction with exhilaration but also with a certain dread. There were things she could say in prose that would be lost in verse—modes of consciousness and nuances of relationship that needed the spacious discursiveness of narrative. Yet she had been earnestly counseled by friends years before to preserve unsullied her reputation for elusive, dryad-like perfection, a reputation won in prewar London where she had been a leading Imagist poet. "H.D." was not just a nom de plume; it was a warranty for exquisiteness. Prose fiction could only succeed in battering her hummingbird wings and send her crashing to the earth where scurried all the other would-be novelists. Defying this advice yet heeding it too, she wrote large quantities of fiction, tucked most of it away in cupboards, destroyed some of it, and offered little to publishers.

What H.D. needed was a way to be printed without being published, a seeming contradiction. The answer came at the beginning of July 1934, when her wealthy companion Bryher, daughter of the British shipping magnate Sir John Ellerman, offered "to have fifty copies only printed of any one of your mss. Think what a lot of type you could burn then." Here was the perfect expedient. Bryher, who was always looking for ways to prod her talented friends into active creation, could also indulge her passion for amateur psychoanalysis: she could play at being literary agent and free her friends from their inhibitions into the bargain. (She was active in promoting psychoanalysis in Britain and gave financial support to a number of well-known practitioners, including Freud.) Bryher settled on the expensive Dijon printer, Maurice Darantiere (whose long-suffering compositors had labored over Joyce's revisions of *Ulysses* a decade earlier). Soon, H.D., Robert Herring, and other intimates were busily preparing manuscripts for Darantiere. There were even hopes of luring Marianne Moore into the Bryher factory.

The complicated circle had arrived at a rare sort of equilibrium. Ringmaster Bryher, high-booted and scarlet-coated, cracked her Freudian whip as her skittish coterie went obediently through its paces. At the end of it all, H.D. had three small volumes to her credit: *Kora and Ka* (1934), *The Usual Star* (1934), and *Nights* (1935; reissued by New Directions in 1986). The neatly printed "booklets" (as H.D. called them), bound in arresting white paper covers, arrived just as she was preparing to leave for Vienna for a second period of analysis with Freud. "This edition of one hundred copies has been privately printed for the author's friends. No copies are for sale," read a note opposite the title page. Recipients included Marianne Moore, Conrad Aiken, Havelock Ellis, Frances Gregg, and Silvia Dobson. Aiken responded quickly. He had enjoyed "Kora and Ka" the most and admired H.D.'s "packing-in of the various levels of awareness or personality, at the same time keeping the narrative vivid and fresh." Other stories he had found "a little too upholstered, too patterned," and he worried that the characters were a trifle leisured and decadent. Yet "what you are doing with *form* interests me profoundly" (letter of 31 October 1934).

But it was Marianne Moore's reaction that really delighted H.D. Characteristically, Moore confessed herself smitten by certain phrases and acutely rendered particulars in the stories, proofs that painful experience had been transmuted into accuracy. "I hope you will never doubt from such worms as myself the admiration which the shining face of your courage evokes" (letter of 15 October 1934). H.D. could not contain her joy. Writing Bryher from Berne en route to Vienna, she crowed, "I have had my first *real* fan letter from a woman—Marianne, of *all* people! . . . I am positively limp!!!! I was terrified of

M.M. And she wrote THE most beautiful letter. Now I repeat: I have YOU to thank for all this, Fido" (28 October 1934). Bryher's stratagem had worked; she had struck upon the perfect halfway house between the prison of unpublished silence and the ordeal of the writers' marketplace. In Bryher's philosophy, private editions did not really constitute publication at all but rather a means of getting rid of a lump of manuscript against the day when the work could appear, recast perhaps, in the ordinary way. Meanwhile, H.D. could take pleasure in a controlled dissemination of her work and (to the horror of present-day scholars) make gleeful bonfires of her drafts and typescripts. Bryher had found a way to unblock her friends.

H.D. soon concluded that her Dijon coup and her second analysis with Freud, both coming in the fall of 1934, marked a turning point in her life. She wrote Bryher towards the end of her stay in Vienna: "The printing of the Ka-s was the beginning of this new regime, and I am grateful to that and don't care much now what happens" (30 November 1934). She often referred to her booklets by some affectionate, bantering term: her "Ka-s," her "Peter Rabbit books," her books of "Br[yher] and the Br press." Late in life, she fetched the small volumes from an attic trunk and found them "very intense and beautifully written," the atmosphere "so living." The stories, she noted, "weave over and through the social-texture of the years when Kenneth [Macpherson] and Bryher and I were together in Vaud, or travelling, or separated as in London. They are subtle stories, difficult to re-read." She added that the tales "enshrined" something of the Bryher and Kenneth of that exhausting, magical period of the late twenties and early thirties ("Compassionate Friendship," 1955).

H.D. wrote the stories of *Kora and Ka* after returning from her first trip to Monte Carlo with Kenneth Macpherson in July 1930. Macpherson was a witty, elegant young Scotsman with a diffuse creative streak who had charmed his way into the lives of Bryher, H.D., and H.D.'s young daughter, Perdita. He became H.D.'s lover and, quite soon thereafter, as if to certify his centrality in the ménage, Bryher's husband. Christian in "Mira-Mare" has some of the detached charisma of Macpherson, and his relationship with Alex (the H.D. figure), though a little disembodied, captures the note of casual warmth and telegraphic repartee that emerges from the letters of H.D. and Macpherson. "Mira-Mare" was written just before their intimacy was shadowed by Macpherson's affairs with young men and his impulsive globe-trotting. It is a light, affectionate tale, far less moody than its diptych companion "Kora and Ka." Macpherson himself remarked on its vivacity in a letter to H.D.: "Darling, it's gorgeous, full of a rippling, heady gayness, lovely happy story that captures those best qualities of the Coast as they have never before been captured" (24 September 1934). Monte Carlo had become the stamping ground for H.D. and her friends, some of whom set to work on their own "Monte" stories. Robert Herring's *Cactus Coast,* printed by Darantiere in 1934, was one of these.

"Kora and Ka" is decidedly more somber than "Mira-Mare," a sort of penseroso to the latter's allegro. The main character, John Helforth, has suffered a breakdown that has forced him to take a leave of absence from his business, the deadening "ferris-wheel" of letter-writing and bean-counting that makes up his personal ring in the hell of London. He thinks of his crack-up as a victory for his "Ka," the shadow-being that lurks inside him, watching its opportunity to take control. In Egyptian mythology, the ka was a "double" or "dweller" born with every person, a kind of literalized soul that survived the death of its host. But it depended for its immortality on the care of the living, requiring to be nourished with food offerings placed in or near the tomb. In the event that the mummy was destroyed, its ka could reattach itself to a statue or effigy of the dead, and even to drawings or sculptures of articles of food. (In Part I, Helforth contemplates "wooden images" of cows and recalls carvings of grape bunches and wild apricots.) In *The Book of the Dead,* formulaic flattery is lavished on the ka: "Homage to thee O my *ka,* who art my period of life!" The ka could become a very trouble-some poltergeist if its needs were not seen to.

Like so many of H.D.'s characters, but perhaps more tragically than most, Helforth is a deeply divided self, and he uses the shorthand of the ka to express the "broken duality" of his being. The fissured, compound ghosts that inhabit "Kora and Ka" do not admit of a straightforward autobiographical reading. Surely there is a touch of Kenneth Macpherson in Helforth. (Robert Herring quickly spotted his friend in Helforth's affected hand and lounge suit.) Kora, Helforth's companion, resembles Bryher in her volcanic temper, her hurt, staring eyes, and her addiction to psychoanalytic clichés. Aspects of H.D. find their way into the two characters as well. Kora's failed marriage and her ambivalences about children and child-bearing reflect H.D.'s experiences in those areas. And Helforth's war phobia, the true source of his breakdown, is modelled on H.D.'s own complex of repressions and traumas stemming from World War I. She lost a brother in that war; Helforth lost two, Bob and Larry, and cannot stop hating his mother for her patriotic zeal in sacrificing her sons. Helforth himself was expected to go, but the conflict ended before he was of age. He might as well have been there, though. His survivor's guilt has crippled him as badly as any wounded soldier returning from the Front (his name hints at "hell-forth"). Stripped of a healthy ego, he feels that he merely "ghosts" for his dead brothers. He is in a sense *their* ka, a shadow fed by his own sorrow and mother-hatred.

Both stories in this volume are products of postwar disenchantment, though they occupy different regions of the European wasteland. For all its lightsome mood, there is a jazz-age ennui and brittleness to the bright watercolor scenes of "Mira-Mare," a touch of cynicism in the dialogues. Its three sections (the afternoon, evening, and night of Bastille Day) follow Alex as she tries to shed her self-consciousness through sensuous plunges in the blue sea and vigorous tourism. Helforth's ego-fragmentation provides the principal structure of "Kora and Ka." The three sections of Part I are narrated by Ka in an abrupt, leering style that protests subservience to Helforth's personality. Part II is in the weary, tortured voice of Helforth himself. Both selves seem to vie for mastery in the shorter Part III; and throughout the story, shifting narrative modes, now first-person, now third, echo the characters' own volatilities. The setting of "Kora and Ka" is uncertain, a place where they speak an unfamiliar kind of French: Switzerland perhaps, or a no man's land of psychic pain. Like "Mira-Mare," this story traces a neat diurnal progression: afternoon, late afternoon, early evening. With *Ulysses* and *Mrs. Dalloway* as powerful models, fiction-writers could abandon temporal sweep for the simple lyrical poignancy of a day's fated progress into night. All of H.D.'s Dijon stories make use of days or nights for their unity of action and mood.

There are suggestions of hope in these two tales, but as often in H.D., these suggestions hover in the realm of myth. Greek and Egyptian stories form a ghostly, billowing backdrop to the characters' lives. Helforth is associated with Dionysus, god of fertility and wine. Early in "Kora and Ka," he studies a grapevine on the barn wall, and his shoes in the grass make him think of "amputated dead feet," a fancy triggered by his war phobia, but also a glance at Dionysus's dismemberment at the behest of Hera (whose husband Zeus had sired the god on Persephone in one version of the myth). Kore or Kora is another name for Persephone, and it seems that Helforth/Dionysus has been drawn to his own Kora partly from the compulsions of his mother complex. Images of cows and serpents, important in Dionysian worship as well as in the cult of Isis, abound in "Kora and Ka"; and in Part III Kora and Helforth sit down to a meal of wine and fruit that has all the resonance of a ritual meal, a kind of last supper presided over by two dying gods. In Greek mythology, Dionysus defies death by being conceived anew (he is the "twice-born" god), and Kore makes her yearly return in the spring from the halls of Hades. Perhaps Helforth, who has been spiritually dead since his brothers went "west," can now, ten years later, come forth from the tomb ("hell-forth" again). Perhaps Kora can conquer her maternal guilt and the bitterness she feels towards her estranged husband, Stamford. "Now we are Kore and the slain God . . . risen," proclaims the narrator (Ka? Helforth?) at the conclusion of the story. Isn't it pretty to think so?

At their deepest level, "Kora and Ka" and "Mira-Mare" are about the mind of the artist. The ka that usurps Helforth's being is undoubtedly a kind of madness, a frighteningly "impersonal way of seeing," a "curse of intimate perception," an "over-mind or other-mind or over-world experience." Yet these are precisely the symptoms that H.D. had long before observed in her own creative self (as recorded in her 1919 essay, "Notes on Thought and Vision"). Alex in "Mira-Mare" escapes her intellect by allowing her senses to respond to sea and sun, in contrast to the self-conscious Christian. Swimming out to her rock, she achieves a state of "forgetting-remembering" and passes into mythopoeic consciousness, travelling back in "sub-aqueous" memory through Europe and America to Paestum and to Philae, island sacred to Isis. H.D. was keenly aware of the risks entailed by this other-mind that made aesthetic creation possible, that eclipsed the John Helforth in her and released the ka. They were risks worth taking. Her "Ka-s," as she lovingly called her little white books, were in a sense her doubles, shadow-souls that would survive her earthly extinction. It becomes our duty, the duty of the living, as prescribed in Egyptian mummy lore, to care for these Ka-s and make sure they do not wander homeless.

A Note on the Text

The text that appears here is a photo-reproduction of the 1934 private edition printed by Imprimerie Darantiere of Dijon. In the 1950s H.D. jotted over two hundred corrections into her copies of *Kora and Ka* (now at the Beinecke Library, Yale). Most of these concern punctuation, but a handful are substantive changes and worth noting here: for "grape-bushes" (11) read "grape-bunches"; for "Kora pushes back" (31) read "Kora pushed back"; for "fed out belching mothers" (36) read "fed our belching mothers"; for "belonging to this minute" (52) read "belong to this minute"; for "sea-pirate sunk back" (65) read "sea-pirate sank back"; for "as old missionary looking dame" (83) read "an old missionary looking dame"; for "a Basque made-up" (84) read "a Basque make-up"; for "platinum grey" (95) read "platinum-blue."

KORA AND KA

VAUD
1930.

I.

1.

There are two things mitigate against me, one is my mind, one is the lack of it. Kora brought me here. She thinks that I am overworked. I am overworked. Kora is exquisite and helpful. I follow her as a child follows its mother. But she is more to me than any mother could be to any child. She is to me what a materialized substance is to a shadow. Without substance, shadow cannot exist. I cannot exist without Kora. But I am more to Kora than a shadow. I am that sort of shadow they used to call a Ka, in Egypt. A Ka lives after the body is dead. I shall live after Helforth is dead.

I look across a space of grass that is the colour of the chiffon scarf that Kora wore last night at dinner. The grass is the colour of tea-roses. From the burnt grass, there is a slight burnt fragrance like tobacco scattered across pot-pourri. The hand of Helforth lies affectedly across the grey knee of his lounge suit. The clothed knee is a dummy knee in a window. The shod feet are brown leather lumps. They rest in the grass like amputated dead feet. The hand of Helforth lives the more markedly for this. It is a long hand, affectedly flung there, living. I, this Ka, cannot see the face of Helforth.

I feel Helforth's eyes. They are glass-grey eyes. I feel his contempt. It is the contempt of integrity, he has worked too hard. I tear, as it were, the curtain that shuts me from Helforth and I feel Helforth's eyes widen. When his eyes have sufficiently stared at that wall opposite, I will look out. At the moment, the eyes of Helforth see in detail, wooden images placed on a shelf, two cows, one painted red, the other black. His eyes are focussed there, they are not wide enough for me yet. He smiles as he notes the red cow has a bell exactly matching in its minute disproportion, those the others wear on the far hill. He sees the red cow, placed at the shuttered window, like a cuckoo out

of its clock. The cows are a trifle smaller than the
two on wooden platforms that the patron's small
child pulls on uneven wood wheels across the flag-
stones. These cows, Helforth notes smiling, have
been carved especially for this purpose, no doubt
by the same wood-carver who cut those various
plaques and plates of grape-bushes and cluster of
wild-apricot, indoors. The cows relate, by this
association, to the house behind Helforth, to the
green and the stark white and the black and the
grey of its interior. Helforth is abnormally sen-
sitive to various interior focal planes of light.

He is sensitive to all light. His eyes widen in
the blinding sunlight and the sun beats down,
incandescent, on his white face. The sun will
sear Helforth's face away and let me come. His
eyes will go blank, staring straight into the light
and mine will see. I wait for Helforth's eyes to
blind out Helforth. Helforth is amused and delight-
ed with the wooden cow and its disproportionate
minute wood cow bell.

Helforth must see everything. And while his
eyes run along a wire where a clematis is trained,
I grow impatient. The eyes of Helforth drink in

the purple of the clematis blossom and gouge out colour of the rose-clematis. The passion of the eyes of Helforth disregards me, waiting. They come to rest, then, on root-stalk of the vine that clambers up the other side of the barn wall. A straggly tendril pulses toward the passion-flower, through the weight of sunlight. The eyes of Helforth follow the twining insistence of the little tendril. It seems now they will be lost for ever in the purple star. But I know Helforth, and I wait for Helforth. His eyes drop again and rest on the spiral of the grape tendril. Then his eyes fall lower on a sheaf of vine-leaves and on one leaf. As his lids fall and as his mind discards the drug-purple of the lordly blossom, I know he knows that I am waiting. His lids droop to blacken out the heady visual memory of rose and purple, and then widen. His eyes rest on the cool young vine-leaves and I come.

2.

I am most at home with Helforth in this green space. The mind of Helforth has seized on one young grape-leaf. The leaf is, just this morning, flattened as if the sun had ironed it out. It still has the tenderness of the young incurved leaves. The leaf is vertebrate. A flawless spine sends out side branches and those again break off into little veins. The flat young leaf blown sideways, insists on inference. Its underside is like the rose leaves that Helforth and Kora exclaimed over, in the smoke-amethyst rose-bowl Kora brought from her room last night, to place on their dining table. Kora had said, "the room lacks something" and made Helforth try to guess what it was.

Last night, it was rainy in spurts. They had drawn the grey stuff curtains that Kora had brought from London with other things of her own, boxes, candlesticks and this sort of glass bowl. Helforth, looking at the glass bowl, knew, now that the bowl was set there, what it was the room lacked. So, Kora will ask a question in words, then answer it in action. She is, herself, oracle and answer. She said, as she stood, looking down at the rose-bowl, "the light from here, is gouged out like a rainbow in a pope's amethyst... stand here, you'll see. The convex bulge at the base, is one huge amethyst." But Helforth does not stand. He sees the grey-rose pulse of the silver of the leaves. Two of the leaves had bent under when Kora put the rose-stems into water. The amethyst tinted clear water in the bowl turns their under-sides, old-silver. Helforth's eyes rest on that silver. He discarded last night, as well as Kora's pope's amethyst, the cluster of blossoms. His eyes discarded the royal-red of the lordly blossom, uncurled Jacqueminot and the half-opened Gloire de Dijon, as just now he discarded the royal purple and the king-rose of the flat wide clematis. His eyes are at rest in silver and in green and in a rotation of silver-green, green-silver.

Colour has rotated in his mind but he now discards it. If he watches colour in his mind, he will be watching . . . to watch anything at the moment is dangerous. Green has been kind. At the moment, it is the one colour that disregards him. Green does not try to snatch back at him, mitigate, suggest billow of open-curtain or red, red, red. Green is most removed from red, from memory and the mole-trap of his office in the city. If he lets go the hold that I have over Helforth, Helforth will begin the old tread wheel and the iron ferris-wheel of Helforth's fatigue will grind, across colour, odour, perception, will crush me beneath it like an iron heel, a glow-worm or just hatched moth, on grit and pebble. If Helforth lets his mind catch in rotation, even the memory of this half hour of crowded perception, his mind will jerk back to all vicissitudes. His mind trod ferris-wheel, trod old, old round of balance and account, of one, two, three, of nine plus seven makes sixteen. His mind rotated to this rhythm, ground round and round, till Helforth forgot man, men, women. Helforth forced Helforth to go on in ferris-wheel of iron circle against an iron grey sky. One day his mind, just casually set in motion, discarded all the preconceived occupations of that mind. He saw the under-manager as under layers of green water, violet-laced and the numbers on his ledger shone violet-laced, nine, six, up through transparent seaweed. Helforth told Helforth, "you must see a doctor."

The doctor said, "shut your eyes, Mr. Helforth." He did so. The doctor said, "open your eyes, Mr. Helforth." He did so. The doctor said, "now is the large A, to the right or the left of the small script ?" He told him. The doctor said, "look at the small O above the circle and tell me if the twin brackets are *in* or *outside* that circle." Helforth saw a sort of chart, placed at some distance from him. The wooden frame, on which the chart was balanced, reminded him of just such an arrangement of wood and cardboard from which he had learned his letters. Helforth said casually, "I will learn my letters." The doctor said, "I asked, was the bracket *in* or *out*" and he shoved the frame thing gradually nearer. As the huge page loomed before Helforth, he felt himself grow smaller. Helforth felt himself draw away, back and back, the length of the doctor's room and out of the wall behind it. Helforth became Helforth, minute at the minimizing other-end of an opera-glass. Although Helforth was miles away, projected into space, Helforth himself sat there. Helforth said tonelessly, "I don't see anything."

The doctor turned a page of the A, B, C, Chart, said, "don't you even see the lines across the blank space ?" Helforth did not tell the doctor what he saw.

A globe rather the shape of the Venetian glass

that Kora had set on the table last night, again reminded Helforth that man was a microbe. He saw a world like a drop of water and himself enclosed in it. It was a green world. Neither the doctor nor that Helforth, drawn graphically out, through the wall, into indeterminate space, was in it. Helforth repeated to the doctor, who seemed to be exacting some form of decisive answer, "I see nothing."

The doctor turned a luminous lamp-ray across the face of Helforth. As that consulting room incandescence made bar and cross-bar across Helforth's haggard countenance, Helforth felt himself returning. From behind Helforth, a ridiculous dangling full-dress Helforth (seen at the wrong end of an opera-glass) rejoined him. Helforth saw Helforth at the other end of the opera-glass, then the two adjusted into one life-size Helforth. Helforth opened his eyes. Helforth saw pursed-forward mouth, chin elegantly shaved, stubble of inconsequential grey-white moustache. The doctor's face was that of an intelligent elderly wire-haired terrier. Helforth did not like terriers, though, from time to time, he endeavoured to adjust himself to them, contemplated racially, through some friend's dog. So he endeavoured to adjust himself to this man. He saw, over the doctor's cloth shoulder, a case holding a stuffed bird and, in a corner, a cluster of speckled birds' eggs, set in brown grass.

The doctor said, "what do you see now ?" Helforth told him about the speckled eggs and the stuffed bird. The doctor said, "nerves ; you must stop work."

3.

Helforth wondered as he stood waiting for a taxi, how he could do that . . . Helforth opened his eyes, saw the barn door and the sunlight and the triangle of sunlight as it lay on the barn floor. A ray of that light had crossed, gold sun-serpent, that barn floor. Helforth sat up. He examined long hands, the palms were less brown than burnt backs. Helforth lifted his throat to guillotine of sunlight. He jerked at the open collar ; let sunlight sink deeper. He rose to his feet. He thought, "have I been sleeping ?" He knew he was and knew he was not sleeping. Helforth slept, Ka watched or Ka was banished and Helforth stared out, calculating, hard-eyed. For a moment, he had been standing at a street corner, waiting for a taxi while speckled birds' eggs, in dead grass, appeared in a plate-glass window. The speckled birds' eggs were the heads of the new importation of French manikins, shaved that year and gilt or silvered over. He thought, "how can I stop work ?" Then as he stepped into the taxi, he said, "yes, I will stop work." He wondered how he could climb out of the ferris-wheel that had been going on for so long. He was dizzy, as he thought of that, and then abstract problem became concrete, how will I step out of this taxi ? How will I manage legs, arms and how will I get at my little change-purse or manage to extract loose change from my pocket ? Will it be easier to reach in for my wallet which is flat and manageable ? Will the taxi man be able to change a note ? He wondered if he were hungry, wondered if the taxi man would think he was drunk. He hadn't smoked for some time.

The taxi stopped with a jerk, beside a pile of wooden building-blocks. The blocks were stacked each side of the road, like neolithic stone-blocks. Beyond the double doorway of neolithic wood blocks, there was a blazing brazier. Helforth saw fire. He thought, "I am cold." It was, he remembered, autumn. There was a mist creeping across the brazier flame, it was incense across an altar. He thought of incense, thought of an altar. He remembered that he had left the stack of letters unstamped and wondered, in neurotic agony, if the office boy would drop them into the post-box, without looking at them. He hadn't been sure of the stamps and had intended to have the lot weighed. They were all of a bulk, the usual quarter-form, sent out to the share-holders. He remembered it was autumn because of the usual form that he had forgotten to stamp, neurotically wracked for fear the boy would just sweep the lot up into his office satchel and not see they weren't stamped.

Now John Helforth, staring at sun-serpent on barn floor, stood up. I stood up. My legs were stiff. My legs were too long. The same legs had been too long that autumn, late afternoon, cramped sideways in the taxi. I had been sitting crouched down, flung down, I now remembered, like a tailor's dummy or a rag doll. I recalled exact panic of mental calculation, how will I get out of this taxi ?

I got out finally because the taxi man poked his head around and said, "the street's up, sir, shall we wait till the traffic block this end's cleared or shall I drive round it ?" Taxi drivers ask these things, lest they be maligned for extorting undue tax. The frayed edges of my mind would not then stand argument. With the frayed edges of my mind, I could not stand up "wait" or "go around" and watch the two naked gladiators fight the thing out. I could not any more stand, watching the contest in the blood-stained sand of my own mind's arena. I got out.

Kora said, "hello." I had to squint close in the town mist to see who it was. I saw chin, nose ; eyes were drawn back under a dark green little sort of helmet. I remembered the hat was green because I remembered thinking her yellow fur, drawn tight across her shoulders and about her hips, made her look like a caterpillar. Or wasn't the hat green ? We have arguments about it.

She said it was mole-grey; she afterwards called the thing *taupe*. (She would say, "how could you think I would wear green with that coat ?") I said, "I must pay this taxi." She said, "O don't. Do keep him. I've been looking for a taxi." Kora and I got into the taxi like a pre-arranged rendez-vous. I said, "where are you going ?"

She didn't seem to know where she was going, didn't seem to care much. I could never watch again the crowded agonies of that blood-strewn arena, the thing my mind was, when I stepped out of a ferris-wheel. But I could watch some one else, wonder, now what exactly is this woman's sort of worry ? Has she too forgotten to put stamps on her letters. I said, "have you forgotten to put stamps on your letters ?"

Kora answered me, as if it were the one question in the whole world she had anticipated. Kora does answer that way. She said, "letters ? I was thinking of letters." She reached into her flat hand-bag, dragged them out. She gave me a little bundle. "Suppose you drop the whole lot in the river," she said. She said, "look at them." I sorted out the letters, just managed to make out, in the blurred light of the taxi window, that they were addressed in the same writing. The writing was decisive, the nib was stub and the down-strokes thick. But the writing was Ninevah to me. She said, "read out the address to me." I said, "I'm afraid I can't. I haven't got my glasses." I never wear glasses but I didn't want to tell her about the doctor and I didn't want to tax my mind to read things. I said, "if it were lighter, I could read them."

I said that evasively, not wanting to mean any-thing. She said, "I haven't had tea, I'm hungry. Can't we get out here ? " We got out. I paid the taxi. We went in a half familiar little side-door, we were in the Bay-tree. Kora said, "just this once, just this once . . . dinner." I said, "why just this once ?" Kora said, "criminals condemned to die, have a last wish haven't they ?" I said, "yes, I think so. But why ?" "Some," Kora said, "ask just for a good meal." I said. "I can't apply anything just now." She said, "I . . . but it's all right since you've got hold of the letters." I said, "I dropped them in the box outside the door here." I said, "I must have done it automatically." She said, "that's done it."

I avoided looking at her over fish and entrée, but watched her lap up her ice like a starved cat. I slipped mine over to her. She never even noticed, went on lapping. Over coffee, I said, "done what ?"

II.

I.

There are two things that mitigate against me. One is my mind, one is the lack of it. I, John Helforth, go on existing in that beam of sunlight. As I stand now, stretching, the bar of light that underlined that triangle, (sun-serpent) is exactly parallel to the threshold of the doorway. Parallels, parallels . . . are two things that travel along, equidistant, and never quite meet. Parallels ? I am John Helforth, I say, yawning and I endeavour to banish, in that yawn's exaggeration, the monster I call, for lazy lack of definition, "Ka." Ka is far off now ; Ka partook of symptom, was neurotic breakdown ; Ka, it is true, led me, made me, having made me, preserved me—but yawning, I say, for what ? If I, Helforth, get rapt back into this Ka thing, contemplating vine-green leaf, Helforth will be good for nothing. There is so much to be done, so much to be thought of ; Kora.

Kora is everything. Without Kora, Ka would have got me. Sometimes I call Kora, Ka, or reverse the process and call Ka, Kora. I am on familiar terms with Kora, with Ka, likewise. We are, it is evident, some integral triple alliance, primordial Three-in-One. I am Kora, Kora is Helforth and Ka is shared between us. Though she repudiates affiliation with Ka, and refuses to discuss it, yet the fact remains. Ka is Kora, Kora is Ka. The waif must be shared between us.

Ka weeps, wails for attention and then must be put to sleep like any tired infant. Though Ka, unhappily it seems, in that too, like most infants, is never really tired. Ka wears me to a shred. It is I who am bone-thin. Soul is, I have proved it, octopus. Nevertheless, octopus cannot devour utterly. I am frame still, albeit, bone and sinew. I stretch arms. They are my arms. I, I am John Helforth.

I stamp feet, John Helforth's feet. Feet are no longer amputated brown lumps lying flat in burnt grass. They are my feet and the shoes are from

Thornton's, Bond Street.   I look at shoes, my shoes.
I remember how I bought these shoes, my parti-
cular shoes.   I will remember.   I will to remember.
For one instant, for some long or short space of
time, memory was eradicated.   Ka brushed across
my mind, a sponge on a slate.   Ka then was the
shape of a drop of water, magnified to the size of a
universe.   Ka was a universe.   In it, I swam, one
microbe in a water-bead.   Kora and I do not talk
of this thing.   Kora says, "forget that."

Kora tells me to forget Ka that, in London, brush-
ed out my mind.   I tell Kora to forget other things.
Kora's eyes strain forward, they are too big and
blue, like bruised flower texture.   They are flower
petal, ruined in soggy down-pour, they are no
longer flower, they are not good stuff, they are not
rain nor sun nor water.   I hate Kora when her
eyes get that poked-out, bruised look.   I will not
look at Kora.   I say, "the kids would stifle you,
after this taste of freedom.   Don't set up lurid iron
bars.   For God, his sake, don't set up iron bars of
memory."   I will to be John Helforth, an English-
man and a normal brutal one.   I will strength into
my body, into my loins.   I say, "for God's sake

Kora, you're crippling your integrity . . . Lot's wife.
Stop thinking of the children.   Anyhow, you don't
really want to see them, it's (to use your own
phrase) guilt-complex."   She turns on me, "child-
ren. You never had a child."   I do not retaliate,
as I well might do.   There are so many things that
I might say at this moment, that I don't say
anything.   I could concentrate everything into
one word, and that word, "Kora."   I don't even
say that.   I don't reach out my hand as I might
do, hand sculptured, she says, of meagre metal, an
Aztec (she says) or archaic edition of Rodin's some-
what bloated (she says) Hand of God.   I do not
say "Kora."

   I do not say "Kora," for why should I ?   I
insist on masculinity and my brutality.   I drag out,
perhaps, tobacco, lift up and let fall disgustedly,
books on a table or upset her work-box.   I de-
liberately do something that Helforth would not
do, could not do.   I become a small lout in my
mother's drawing room and let resentment flare
up, I remember Bob and Larry, hating each equally
for their several betrayals.

   I let red flares eat out my mind, red Verey light

shall burn up Ka who is a jelly fish, who is a microbe, who is (a specialist all but told me) a disease. I will burn away my soul with my mind, or should I say my body ? I have a right like any man, like any woman, like any other ill-begotten creature, to a body.

Who gave me this broken duality ? Who gave me this curse of intimate perception ? I curse Ka. I say, "I hate you, Kora ; when your eyes go poking forward, you are really ugly." I look at Kora as she stands, looking down into the courtyard where that wretched child is pulling its wooden cow on the wooden platform, making the uneven wooden wheels vibrate, dot and tick of some wretched S.O.S. between himself and Kora. I say, "I'd like to smash that kid and its wretched wood cow. Anyhow, I've had enough of cows for one lifetime." I underline cow, spew out, "cow, cow, cow, mother-love or mother-lust I call it." I say, "this cow passion is the disintegrating factor of modernity. I mean you and your sort keep back the world." I say, "mother, mother, mother," and I say, "Larry."

I have meant to be robust ; I have meant to smash furniture. I find myself seated on the low rush-bottomed arm-chair. I beat my hands on its sides. I say, "everything in this damn place is rushes and wood and cow, cow, cow." I say, "when are we going back ? I can't stay here forever." It is her turn, at this moment, to retaliate, she does not. Then I sway. Ka is coming ; there is green of a pale grape tendril. I hear a voice, it is only Kora but still I say, "Ka shan't get me." I regret temporary weakness, I am strong again, I say, "rushes and reeds and cows." I say, "your mother complex is ugly, Kora. You look into yourself with those ugly poked-out eyes, like a beggar, in Naples, cashing-in on siphilitic scars." I go on, I say, "cow," I say, "mother, mother, mother." Then I fling myself down, anywhere, head on the table, or head that would beat through the wooden floor to the rooms that lie beneath it, "Larry."

2.

Kora knows, the specialist knows, everybody knows that if I had said this ten years ago, I might

now be all right. Kora knows and Kora will not
retaliate, at least not now, not while I beat my
head actually or metaphorically on the floor . . .
I look up, I am really standing in bright sunlight,
finishing out a yawn with an extra gape and a gulp
like a fish, all but caught on a fish-hook. I disen-
tangle fish-hook. I see where I stand. One foot
is on brown grass, the other half is shoved in,
against a cottage garden border of fire-blue lobelia.
Sweet-alyssum ought to be there too ; who plants
lobelia without sweet-allysium ? I remember my
mother's garden, her drawing room. I remember
Larry. The doctor told Kora if I could have
remembered sooner . . . I ask myself, who is
Larry ? I should never have talked to Kora. I
would never have told Kora, if she had not licked
up that ice, in the Bay-tree, like a starved cat.
I hate suffering in animals. I used to walk round
and round the squares in London, to escape child-
ren. I do not like children. I do not like cats.
When Kora pushes back the second plate in the
Bay-tree and said, "yes, coffee," I knew decisively
that she was more cat than caterpillar. I said to
her, "you are more cat than caterpillar." It was

the sort of remark that, in Bob, would have been called "whimsical." Larry and I used to practise at Bob being "whimsical."

Mother could have kept Larry at home. I was too young. Larry was of course vicious to have told me, in precise detail, all that he did. It was a perverse sort of sadism. I loved Larry. I would have gone on, loving men and women if it hadn't been for Larry. How could I love anyone after Larry ? My mother used to say, "*Bob* would have been too noble-minded to have regretted Larry." Bob ? But Bob went that first year, dead or alive he was equally obnoxious. He was the young "father," mother's favourite. I was sixteen. By the time I was ready, the war actually was over. Mother reiterated on every conceivable occasion, "Larry is only waiting to get out there." I don't know what mother thought "there" was. It was so near. It was "here" all the time with me. Larry was sent to avenge Bob, I was to be sent to avenge Larry. It was already written in Hans Anderson, a moron virgin and a pitcher. We were all virgin, moron. We were virgin, though Larry saw to it that I was not. Larry.

I, John Helforth, kick at a scrubby little border of lobelia. I hear a voice call "Helforth." I scowl out, under hard blue eyes. There is no Ka anywhere now visible. There is Kora standing on the uneven flag-stones, she says, "tea is ready. What were you doing all this time here, sleeping ?" I say, "yes, Kora, sleeping." Ka has gone off. He lives in water and I say, "I'm going to-morrow up toward Grangettes to get you water-lilies." Kora is looking better. Her eyes are lobelia-blue, fire-blue now in her burnt face. Her arms are the colour of the chiffon scarf that she wore last night at dinner. The hollow in her neck is as fragrant as tobacco and her flesh tastes, I tell her, of water-lilies and of pears. She says, "water-lilies and pears . . . what a mutinous sort of salad," and I say "for God's sake, don't be whimsical."

My shoes are too heavy. I must get a pair of light ones or some sort of sand-shoes. What can I get here ? Kora has pulled off stockings ; women always have half and half sort of things to suit any odd occasion. Her low-heeled one-strap shoes are of soft café-au-lait leather. Her ankles above them and her bare legs are just one shade lighter. She

33

has really gone a sort of honey-colour. I wait for some sort of opening to tell her, before I forget, that she is honey colour. I pull off an apposite spray of honey-flower that seems, telepathically, to have forestalled me. "Honey-flower," I say as I tickle her behind the ear, "is a prettier word than honey-suckle." "Is it ?" says Kora. We can argue this sort of thing out, endlessly.

She blows out electric spark of the burner and pours my tea. "Now," says Kora, "you are back in London ; you are having your first affair ; you are happier." . . . I look at Kora ; I see no wide blue of fire-blue lobelia but a camelia that has opened under the touch of Larry. I see Jean and I see Larry. I wish Kora wouldn't be so blatantly and conspicuously tactful. I know the doctor told her not to let me slip out into a sort of impersonal way of seeing. I know they told her to drag out things, to make me talk, to make me tell things. Well, I will tell things, "Kora."

"Darling ?" "This is not London. This is no first affair. If you are trying to get me to talk about Larry, well you will do. Larry would have withered you with a pseudo-sarcastic whimsicality

34

as he did everyone but Jeanette. Larry did not love Jeanette, she did not love him. They clung together in a world that was made for them, a world of flickering lights and long corridors," (I fling about my rhetoric) "of single floating wicks in glass lamps, of music behind curtains and of wind in country gables. There was a world made for Larry, there was a world made for Jeanette" (here my breath dramatically catches) "and it was taken from them. Kora, who took it from them ? Was it you, was it me ?" (I pause forensically.) *"It was our Mother."*

This may or may not have been true. I don't think poor madre, personally, prevented wicks from floating in glass lamp bowls or wind from howling in country gables. But mother had become symbol. I should have seen it sooner. I had, in Kora's language, "inhibited" the fact that Larry really need not have gone so early. I blamed mother for the death of Larry and I was not noble like Bob. Kora declares that I was in love with madre and that Bob taking the place of father, was my rival. Fantastic explanation yet gives us topic of conversation over our little dinners. One has to talk at dinner. Kora says my attitude is fantastic and linked up with mother-complex. I say I do not think so. I explain it lucidly, as if she herself were a complete outsider, and herself had never heard of that war. I demonstrate how, systematically, we were trained to blood-lust and hatred. We were sent out, iron shod to quell an enemy who had made life horrible. That enemy roasted children, boiled down the fat of pregnant women to grease cannon wheels. He wore a spiked hat and carried, in one hand, a tin thunderbolt and, in the other, a specialised warrant for burning down cathedrals. He was ignorant and we were sent out, Galahad on Galahad, to quell him. His men raped nuns, cut off the hands of children, boiled down the entrails of old men, nailed Canadians against barn doors. . . and all this we heard mornings with the Daily Newsgraph and evenings with the Evening Warscript. The Newsgraph and the Warscript fed out belching mothers, who belched out in return, fire and carnage in the name of Rule Britannia. I said, "Kora, go back to London. What is the matter with you ? Forget sometimes that you are a mother."

36

3.

Kora has a look in her eyes that means sure death. I say "fire away, old die-hard." There is a look in Kora's eyes that does not go with a green helmet and a caterpillar coat. It goes, she is right, with grey and with a sort of undressed leather primitive pelt or polished steel-edge aegis. I say, "when you look like that I understand old Stamford." Stamford was, or I suppose I should say, *is* Kora's husband. I had vaguely known Kora Morrell. I think I had seen her as one of those window-dressed brides who carry out-of-season lilies. Bob was to have been a brother-officer sort of property of Stamford's at that wedding. Bob was otherwise engaged about then ; even Larry was not available. I "ghosted" for them both, soon, veritably, to take on that rôle for life.

When Larry went I, in some odd manner, went "west" with him. It was my feet that were severed . . . a mule's intestines . . . but I must stop this. The doctor said if I could encourage the

37

sub-conscious to break into the conscious . . . but there is a limit even to that . . .

It is Larry, at last analysis, I say, who is responsible for my mind. He shouldn't have told me about Runner 32, as they called him . . . and those others. We had some mad idea of sharing things, life, war, love finally. I didn't stop to reason nor think. I was the half of Larry. That half gone, I too went. I did what I presumed Larry would have done, if he had been left in my place. I took on the rôle of Robert, I was to go in his place. It was the only thing to do, I had not the courage to begin over on my own. I had not the heart to be debonnaire. That word had lost integrity like a worm-gnawed apple. "Debonnaire," "whimsical" were words rotted at the core. Larry had been "debonnaire" at the last, I am certain and old Robert, true to type, no doubt was no end "whimsical."

I never stopped to reason, to think. One does not reason, walking above a torrent on one thin plank. I did not realize that *nothing* depended on me, that a row of aunts was choros out of Hades, that the "family" was only another name for

warfare and sacrifice of the young. I did not in
the least realize that it would be a sort of crime if
mother ("our" mother) did not have her lilies-of-
the-valley on this and that occasion. Such were
my erotic orgies, lilies for my mother. There was
also the birth-day and the death-day of a father
and two brothers. Around these days, aunts stood
like crows, waiting their turn at carrion. It was
not Larry who had been picked by vultures nor
was it Robert. I began to curse Larry, to curse
Bob. Because of their casual and affable "sacri-
fice," I was left, flung high and dry.

Kora looked at me in hatred, the lobelia blue
burnt to a fire blue in her eyes. Then there is no
fire in her eyes. She had touched me on the quick
with Larry. I will do the same with her brats.
Her children are at school now, I will tell her what
happens to small boys at school, things that happen-
ed to me, to Larry. Her eyes are steel. I will
break through Kora for I hate her. I hate all
women because of mother and because of . . .
Jeanette. I say, "you don't look the least like
Jeanette."

Kora says, "what has Jean Drier got to do with me now ?" I say, "you remember you sat there, you blew out the flame, you poured my tea. You said, 'now you are back in London, you are having your first love affair.' You remember you said that." Kora says she remembers. I say, "don't treat me like Bobby or Jo. Keep your brats out of it. I am not Bobby, look tootsie ottsie, mummy's mended your bear. I don't want your teddy-bearizing of this situation." Kora says, "go on." She settles down to it ; she reaches for her work-box. "I don't want this eternal prodding down, I tell you, Kora, this new sort of analysis stuff can't get round the fact of Ka. I know more than any of these nerve-specialists. How can they treat me ? If any one of them had had this over-mind or other-mind or over-world experience, I would listen." Kora says quite steadily, "isn't your over-world as you call it, simply substitution ?" I say, "for what ?" She says, "for this world." I say, "you ask me, then, to accept this world ? You are eternally compromising." She is running flat elastic round the top of one of those tailored knickers. I say, "I like your knickers, Kora. I liked Jean's but then that hardly counted. Do you know, Kora, my mother used to snatch her under-things out of the way, such things too, when she saw any of us boys coming." Kora held up the silk tailored knickers for my inspection. "O, John," she said, "the poor, poor, poor old darling." I have not heard Kora speak that way of my mother. She looks up now, across the pile of fawn and puce and light taupe things that she's mending. "O Johnny," she seldom calls me Johnny, "don't you see what a mess you make of all this ? Can't you just *love* your mother ?" I turn on Kora, I will spew out fire and brimstone, I say "Larry." "O don't, don't, Johnny, that's over." She says, conclusively, that the war is over. "How can it be—when Larry ?" "You," said Kora, "are really as bad as all the fire-eating Anglo-Indians. You go on, you go on with it. Can't you see the flowers growing and ignore the grave-yard ?" "What flowers . . . " I take the taupe bit of silk thing from her. "Ours... Johnny."

III.

I.

Colour has rotated in his mind but he now discards it. His eyes are at rest in silver and in green and in a rotation of silver-green, green-silver. He sees a space of long room with a low ceiling. He sees the curtains Kora had drawn, now open. He sees Kora (in a chiffon sort of robe), draw aside the curtains. He sees shadow wavering across diminished sunlight and sunlight filtering through diminished green. He sees shadow wavering slightly like fern-fronds under water. He sees that the red and blue cluster of field flowers, stamped on the chiffon that Kora has drawn on, lie here, there, across bare arm, bare shoulder, the gallant little bulge her back makes, like field flowers, flung on to a statue sprayed with water. The chiffon robe is light, rain-colour or the texture of a sprayed-out garden fountain. The flowers seem to lie along the shoulder of Kora as if she had been rolling in a meadow. I see Kora as she steps into a pool of sunlight that is stippled over with leaf-shadow. Her feet are bare. They are whiter than her legs and the strap of her shoe has left a white strap on her foot. Her bare foot is shod in a whiter sheaf of white flesh. I see that the strap on the other foot is also white.

Colour has rotated in my mind and dissociation of ironclad idea. My mind was bound in, bound me in a little iron car of ferris-wheel perception. I went round or seemed to go round but all the time my mind, that seemed to lift me above earth, just as inevitably swung me down, back to it. I realize the triviality of that set of perceptions, think of the quarrel we have just had, think rather of a quarrel we had long, long ago before the curtains shut out sunlight as now the curtain lets in filtration of a green diminished shadow. When Kora drew the curtain, it was drawn, dramatically, across a sun-steeped late afternoon. Now Kora opens the curtain and it is still light but (almost imperceptible difference) early evening and not

43

late afternoon. We could not have been there together on the low couch, an hour at the outside, three quarters of an hour, maybe. In that short sector of time, the world altered, slowly, slowly life drew off . . . life drew away, turgid stream, dragging with it silt and bed-rock of grinding memory. Kora was right then. It was right to prod and jab up surface anger. Surface anger can be got at, can be demolished with a like flare of anger. Kora's anger is not like Helforth's anger, but it allays and stills it. But Kora was not really angry. On the surface, Kora tells me she was angry. She sits beside me, she says, "must we ever be angry again, Helforth ?" I say, "Kora it's like this. If I could have had bouts of resentment, anger, hatred, all through those ten years, these great volcanic break-downs wouldn't happen." Kora says, "yes, Helforth. I too. If I could have hated Stamford, known what he was, if I could have loathed him, I might have loathed the children." I take the small hand, it is clothed with a brown glove as if someone had lightly varnished it and lightly passed the brush up, toward the shoulders. I slip the chiffon from the shoulder

44

and am half surprised when the cluster of print-poppies and corn-flowers slips off with it. I say, "you are a bit indecent this way. As if you had on long brown gloves and a silly little throat thing, a thing my mother used to call a 'dickie' in our wash suits." I pull back the chiffon stuff and cover the discrepancy with the print-poppies and blue corn-flowers. I take Kora's hand, almost as if I had not ever kissed her. I say quite solemnly like an apology or a pledge, "you must think better of me. I hate the children, not because they are your children, not even because they are Stamford's. I hate them because they made you suffer." She stares straight ahead now; a small hard little profile cuts against fern shadow and the evening afterglow as it filters through those trees. The feather clouds seem to have slipped like fish through the meshes of those trees, they lie, in light pattern, on the floor, they swim about the quaint strapped-over, bare feet like a swarm of gold fish. The shadows are gold-fish and rose-fish, from some Japanese aquarium. I say, "forgive me, Kora."

Her profile is hard. Sometime, somewhere, there was a jab, a sort of slice was taken out of Kora.

You feel a certain sort of tenderness was removed, as one might have one's appendix removed, on an operating table. The stability of Kora is not really stable. It is the stability of a frozen rabbit that hears the hounds not far off. She seems to be listening, to be waiting. "But Kora, they can't ever take the children." She does not accept me, she is looking far off. She says, "it's odd. I would never have minded, none of it would have mattered, if I had ever loved him." I say, "Kora you did love him." I say even, "you do love him." I feel with one last flagrant tendril that binds me to the past, that this is somehow what Larry would have said. I have forgiven Larry, now, for dying and even as I said, "I will let Larry go," Larry stood there near me. I feel, "this is what Larry would have said to Jeanette." I feel with one last fibre that binds me to that past, that I must now (having discarded Larry) be once more with him, just this once, this once, Larry. I say, "you do really, Kora, love him."

My eyes are filmed over. I feel, in death, only the tenderness of dismissal. Kora has done this for me. Well, Kora reconciled me to death, I, appositely, will try to reconcile her to life. Kora has told me how she loved the children, she will go back to them. "Kora, you have only to go to them." Her arms are round me, a terrible vice clutches, presses (octopus) breath from my body. I am frightened at this very sudden turn, this octopus-like clutch of those arms below my chest, crushing breath out. I am frightened at the strength and the intensity of those small arms. They are wire and fibre, they bind close, close. I bracelet her two wrists with my hands, I do not draw off those wrists. She lets go suddenly. She slips from me, lies on the floor ; the print-poppies make poppy and corn-flower pattern on her back. I am amazed to see poppies and cornflowers convulsed, shaken like field flowers under high wind or down sweep of sharp scythe. Something has been cut down, it lies gasping among those silver and rose-fish from a Japanese aquarium. "Kora." It is Kora lying there, gasping in her agony, among rose-fish and gold-fish that have now merged into one blur of shadow. In the shadow, the soft folds of chiffon stuff now lie still.

I stoop. I lift her up, a drowned girl from the water.

"But Kora darling, love is always like that."
I have lain her on the couch, smoothed the poppies
round her, kissed her. "But Kora darling . . ."
I am puzzled. Kora has been married ten years,
has twice been a mother. I cannot imagine what
has hurt her. I go back to Larry. I remember
what Larry said of Jeanette, "her husband is that
sort of plough-boy who lies heavy on a woman."
I didn't understand. It occurred then to me that
men were like that but they were plough-boys, they
precisely were not gentlemen. It had never occur-
red to me that such things happened among ordin-
ary even presentable sort of people. I tried to
explain, tried to keep her quiet, stop her gasping,
stop her endlessly, endlessly repeating, "it wouldn't
have mattered all the hideous mutilation, if just
once, just once, I had known—this."

2.

We had the padrone's niece bring the tray up-
stairs again. Kora explained in the sort of French
we talk here, "Monsieur is tired out," vaguely

indicating papers, profusion of books and note-books, "writing." My writing has been a symbol and a myth. We hold to it ; I am writing. I will not have invalidism thrust on me but it is Kora does the writing. She had straightened the couch cover, flung down books there and her note-books. She has neglected the cushions, re-covered with some of her stuff from London. There was a print in the dull gold one, like a marble head in velvet. I found myself surreptitiously smoothing over that print of Kora's heavy small stone head. The heavy stone head and the various bits of marble, foot, hand and severed torso had been re-assembled. Kora had gone to bits ; it seemed as if each separate bit of her, had needed re-adjustment, as if I must say over and over, to hand, to thigh, to line of tortured eye-brows, "it's all right. Love is this." I had not kissed her, after that first kiss of my condonation as I smoothed red poppy-heads about her. I condoned not this present lapse but the fact that, till now, she had astonishingly hidden the fact that she had not loved me. I had simply thought her proud and reserved. I remembered Jeanette saying, "I never gave myself to anyone

49

but Larry." At that time, I had considered Jean infallible, a woman older even than was Larry. I had taken Jean and Larry as final court of appeal, in the sheer technique of loving, and with final severance, my own bruised being had accepted things as they were. Looking at Kora, as she sat with the circles from the lamp shade, dramatically, insisting that the ear-ring and the chin were an anomaly, I realised that, but for Larry, I might have gone on . . . not understanding anything. I realized that my odd dissociation had left me free and that the ten years were not wasted. I said, "Kora, that jade ear-ring doesn't go with pre-fifth Attica."

Her hand went up to her ear. She looked at me across a space of white cloth. On the cloth, arranged out of a Flemish gallery, were two tumblers with bulbous cups, with stocky rooted stems and solid bases. One tumbler lay at my right, one placed exactly, like the Grail, in front of Kora. "Take, eat," I said and shoved the flat plaque toward her. To-night, it held a pseudo mondaine assortment of "town" fruit, bananas, of all things, and some oranges. I said, "what has happened to

the cherries ?" and Kora answered, "I imagine they
think we like change. We had cherries last night,
and we had cherries at noon." "I seem to dis-
believe in those bananas, they strike some wrong
note. It reminds me of a restaurant in Soho where
I once took Jeanette after we'd seen off Larry."
Now when I say Jeanette, Larry, I am one with
them, we are of one age, there are four of us here.
I do not say "Larry" now with that back-fire of
resentment. I see mother sitting far off ; she
should be an American mother, from the back of a
magazine, sitting in a rocking chair. I say, "I
seem to be American. I see mother in a rocking
chair." Then I see Kora as something flagrant
herself, out of a bright painted advertisement,
as she lifts the flat plaque and calls through the
open door in the sort of French we talk here,
"Hedweg, Monsieur would like again the cherries."
Hedweg comes back with cherries, a marionette
pulled in on a wire. She takes the bananas, does
not seem perturbed about it. She probably her-
self, for a change, would like bananas.

I say, "Kora, you started some time back, before
you drew the curtains, while you were running

flat elastic in your knickers, to give me one of your admirable treatments." It is as if I had flicked a little whip in her face. I had not meant to be ironical. Something in one, instinct of defence, protection, incredibly stupid habit, made that tone flick in her face. I had not meant to be ironical, had not really linked up that Kora yet with this one. Seeing her, with her half-emptied goblet, a Grail, before her, I had not thought that anything I could say would now seem incongruous to her. It seemed now that Kora had second sight but Kora had not. I expected her to see through my remarks as I myself see through them.

Ka, it appeared however, still belongs to Helforth, his personal little dragon; it seemed, with the assistance of this personal little pest, that I could see around and, as it were, through walls and into tree-trunks. I could see through the wall behind Kora and I saw Kora sitting in a Florentine frame, her head encompassed with an aura of lilies. I saw Kora then just as the Kore-Persephone and I realised that I too have proper affinity with her. I see that all this turn of chin and inapposite jade ear-ring, belonging to this minute, to me and postwar Kora and to dead Larry. Larry was dead, dead, dead, wail O Adonis, but Larry wasn't that youth. Larry was the young Dionysus, tramped to filth with the sacrificial entrails of dead mules, likewise slain for the whole world's atonement and the horror that had so often rasped me at the thought of those Alsatian dogs that ran, for their young Saxon masters, straight into the Allies' gunfire, was appeased strangely. "Dogs and horses, Kora," I said "and Larry."

I could feel Ka across my forehead like a hand placed there. I saw the Grail, I saw Kore-Persephone, I saw goblets out of a Venetian gallery and fruit now off a Flemish platter. I saw the planes of the wall, like the perspective in Tintoretto, and I saw red fire and incense across an altar. I said, "that day, I ran across you, Kora, I saw incense across an altar. It was one of those red braziers, you know, they melt tar in . . . You had a fur like a caterpillar. You had on a green hat." Kora looked up, reduced now to a portrait, in a subsidiary French room, in an art gallery. With a cherry between her teeth, she had, at that moment, a somewhat blatant prettiness ; now she is French.

Her cheeks are brushed with rose, her eyes are French-blue, exaggerated with soft shadow. Kora says, "it wasn't a green hat but a grey one."

I am willing to admit, now, that it was a grey one. Admitting even that technically the hat had been green, it must have been in that mist and underground etched-in sort of city, smudged in with so dull a green smear that, for process of to-day's comparison, it might have been grey. I see Kora now standing, by the sooty iron railings, and a tree etched above her with metallic outline and the smoke, from beyond, mingling with the grey mist. I realise one tone, no mist can smudge out, I remember the fire embers of that brazier, as promise of a fire that had not then sprung between us. We were Kora of the Underworld and Dionysus, not yet risen. I was then Larry and those others, had no place then in any living landscape. Now we are Kore and the slain God . . . risen.

MIRA-MARE

VAUD
1930.

I.

Mira. Mare. Miramare. A pencil traced words in a pocket diary. The blue suède covers were worn, the pages were headed with inept dates ; it was a pocket-diary she had discarded as one does discard pocket-diaries, post-dated three years. Then she had scraped it up from somewhere, scratched out an ancient laundry-list, jotted down train time. The volume had been spared for that pencil. The pencil, almost virgin, still fitted beautifully. The tiny pencil fitted, with clean minute bevelled edge, into the suède loop. The loosened pages fluttered now, broken gilt, as Alex shut the volume. The pages were gilt-edged. Gilt-edged securities. She wanted this security.

The place smelt of paint. The boy said, "no, madame. Yes, but madame, the apartments run from 13,000 francs." He repeated the 13,000.

The girl had already written it in the note book. Alex fluttered open the post-dated pages to be sure again the girl had written it. The girl was standing; she said, "we'd better call him up now." The boy said, "no, it's the 14th. He won't be in the office." Alex said, "yes, July 14th. I am here on visit. Monsieur is now waiting for me. If you will give me the—the *thing*, I will go. I will come back. I will come back to-morrow—" "At eleven," the girl said. The boy said, "at ten." Alex noted the boy wore a perforated white pull-on, punctured regularly like a sieve. His dark hair stood up on separate wires, his eyes were not blue enough in his pale face. Yet she saw his point. He was, in a small way, another of what Christian called, "beach-bums." The padrone and herself and a hypo-thetical monsieur and a conference at eleven, that might be late, would spoil his day. Her flat wide eyes caught blue in his, none too blue. She said, "at ten. Monsieur cannot be later. To-morrow is our last day." Her smile was for the boy who jerked up loose trousers about thin flanks.

Paddy said the French tried for places like this, would take anything, these Bretons. The boy was ill, was janitor. There were three doors, Alex noted as she passed through the middle one. She flicked open the flat suède covers to read again, Monsieur le Colonel Darso. It sounded more Italian than French, a bastard tongue, this Monagesque. She read Miramar, Bd. des Moulins from 13,000 francs. The girl had spelt it Miramar. But the letters carved on the stone coping at the stairs' foot, read Mira-Mare. Alex turned to stare at them. M-i-r-a she spelt, to make certain; the Wonderful. She ran her fingers, Braille fashion round the letters. The Wonderful; she read M-a-r-e. It was obvious you must pronounce that last *e*, *a* Italian, though the way the girl wrote it, was French. Miramar didn't mean anything, it must be Mira-Mare. But French or Italian, it was much the same thing here in Monte Carlo. She thought of Monaco as a bastard little principality, stuck like a beauty-patch, on the face of Europe. Europe wore its Monte Carlo like a beauty patch, humourously and out of fashion. Mira the beautiful, Mare the Sea, obviously.

She hunched the "thing" under her right arm. This "chose" was an exaggerated towel, rolled tight, containing shoes, cap, swimming suit. The cap was slate blue, the shoes were cobalt, shining paint-box blue. The cap fitted like a Lindburgh helmet. She stepped carefully in sandals that had loosened at the heel, in five days. Five days ago, the low-heeled, wicker-work, Deauville sandals had been snug, had fitted. In a few days, if she could have stayed, she would have managed without stockings. The trouble was keeping them up. Stockings, half way up the thigh, clipped tight with four garter straps, were a sort of obscenity. In the whole world, there was nothing obscene she felt, but her garter belt, an anomaly.

Alex slid forward with slightly racing movement. She should almost float down these steep stairs ; each step shelved into a low sloping separate plat-form ; each stone required one or two steps or three mincing steps. Her feet moved differently. Every movement of foot, hand, thigh, body, was a fresh invention. She had not felt feet curl under, this way, in years. She thought, "I haven't used my feet like this since I was—since I was a child."

She remembered that she hadn't been happy like this since childhood. And remembering back, she remembered that, then, she had not been too happy. A child is not too happy. She had never been happy, she thought, equally in spirit and body like this. She had been happy with one, with the other, not both. She had never been happy like this, in her life. Happiness was a new garment, fitted her like her Lingburgh helmet. It was snug, fitted her like her paint-box blue rubber beach shoes. She said under her breath, "I am perfectly happy."

The gates, at the railway crossing, were, as usual, slammed tight. The first one could be pushed open with automatic knee. She picked her way across the track, looking right, left. She had not yet seen a train pass. She supposed trains did pass or there would not be these gates. Safe against the second gate, her eyes drugged themselves on more blue ; a glorified morning-glory made a burnt tree blossom. The burnt tree, with unfamiliar spider leaves, was drenched with a new variant on blue, this very dark blue, "paint-box blue," she said again ; her mind would seek no new word, would not forfeit privilege. For the first time now in years (ten ?) her mind was subservient to her. She realised that her mind was subservient ; she let thought stand separate from her, like steel barred sluice-gates. Thought was steel, was platinum, was silver-coloured sluice-gates. Those gates stood wide open. Through her mind, sensation poured, drowning. Pressed away from the rails against the second railway gate, she felt it give before her. She let the gate slam back, with its own weight. Her feet were crunching tobacco-shaped, dried magnolia leaves. Christian said that they were not magnolia. She turned the corner where palms made Egyptian pattern on a wall. The road that made exact perpendicular with this wall, was a dusty common-place engineer's perfection. The new walls, the tunnel, the whole length of magnificent boulevard was punctuated now and again with date, epigraph, such and such a stone and the arms of the Princelet. The wall, the outer wall, the tunnel, appeared scrubbed, new stone. Below the new wall, there were heaps of builders' rubbish ; beyond, patches of apparent refuse, dumps. The sea came in, in low even breakers, like the Atlantic.

The tunnel was cool. Alex overtook the three girls in the new unfaded kimonos and the paper sunshades. They were earlier to-day, rather it was she, delayed at Miramare, who was later. She passed them, bending slightly forward to catch up the few minutes she had lost.

The usual cars stood outside the shaded huts of the garden pavillon, Larvotto. She and Christian had decided that the Larvotto people were not really "snobs" like the exaggerated types that drove restless cars disdainfully past them, toward the Monte Carlo (ipse) Plage, another half mile distant. By "snobs" they meant something mildly different. The Larvottos were not haughty people. They skipped ropes, swung weights, browsed in the private shade of their private palm trees or did intricate dance steps on the sun-lit raised platform. Larvotto people even slid through the chicken wire that vaguely separated goats and sheep. Larvotto patronized their breakers. They were on good terms with Larvotto whose sea-rosemary hedges perfumed their stretch of boulders. Larvotto with sea-rosemary and skeleton eucalyptus was at their right ; beyond them, the Plage line, at their backs, the high wall of the villa, *"the* villa, in excelsis," Christian called it.

Christian was not yet here. A sea-pirate was doing physical jerks behind their rocks. His bathing drawers hung loose, his one-two-three-four was limp, his bare feet slithered as he did fragile knee-bends, his naked shoulders, baked adequately, served only as bone-rim for the basin shape between them. He was lava-baked mummy from Pompeii, doing one-two-three-four, slithering with weak feet on their stones. Now why had he chosen their rock ? It occurred to Alex, immediately, that probably his was the prior claim. In less than a week, she and Christian had become ownerful, arrogant. Now that people couldn't really tell them from the others (they flattered themselves unduly) they belonged here. The palm shadows on the villa-in-excelsis wall moved perfunctorily, like paper cut-out shadows. Christian said, "hello."

She said, "hello, Chris, did you get the money at the bank ?" He nodded, his towel already slung across their rock. She said, drawing nearer, "there's—someone—" and Christian said loudly, "damn." The head of the sea-pirate emerged, jack-in-the-box, and trembled as he balanced on weak toes, then the sea-pirate sunk back. Christian jerked off his coat. The pocket bulged. "You can't leave all our hotel money in your pocket." He fumbled, handed her the packet. Now what good did that do ? She jerked open her zip-bag and stuffed the thing in there. Now why had she screamed at Christian, "did you get the money at the bank ?" He was already in his knitted pull-on, the shoulder straps tucked in at the waist.

She regarded the beach, resenting the zip-bag and the roll of bank-notes. The usual bronze was perched on the usual rock-peak that divided their stretch. It was a bit sandier at and beyond the rock, there were fewer boulders that end, but this side was wilder, as a rule, less crowded. The habitués were already stretched out, a shoal of brown seals ; here and there, one young herd-leader, perched on an outstanding pinnacle. She squinted, drew together wide blue to make out that one. Yes, it was their favourite, hardly to be distinguished, at this distance, save for his electric blue waist band. He wore nothing, a platinum-coloured rubber cap and that blue strip at his waist, and sometimes, his beach-sandals, his "winged sandals," Christian called them. He sat, ran, dived, swam, each a separate entity. Their "favourite" was seen through prism glasses, never one, a varigated gallery. He sat, one of his pet poses, regarding nothing, far to lee.

Her narrowed squint widened like a camera shutter. Light filtered in ; she saw the far beach. They had kicked out their "store" shoes, as she called them, that first day, curious to see what lay beyond the familiar stretch. They were rewarded, for lack of faith in the herd instinct, with broken shins, cactus scratches, the fact that the further beach was more or less dedicated to a row of squalid bungalow huts, concealed this end and from the distant fashionable "plage" ipse, by flowerless oleander, dusty sea-rosemary and thorn-like bundles of dried gorse. There seemed to be a dead stream runnel. One fisherman was perched on the dividing wall that possibly ran, for some sordid purpose, on out toward deep sea. They decided the seals had already pegged out the best ground.

They would follow from now on, herd instinct.
They imagined a mild chuckle from the seals, on
their return, though none spoke. No seal looked
at them for some days. Then, seals looked. She
had plunged to the nearest of the far rocks and had
meant to sun herself nonchalantly on the furthest
to-day, but here was that packet.

Christian wouldn't come with her out to the far
rock. He was afraid of arms, not so brown as
those arms, of back not so bronze and muscular.
Incandescent mind, too, had gone from Christian.
He was young male among other young males,
many of whom, indeed most of whom, were brown-
er. Why, just as they were being formally re-
ceived into this herd, must they go back ?

Damn the damn packet. She tied her dress
round her square bag, stuffed the two into her hat,
weighed down the hat, either side, with shoes. This,
she carefully perched on the flat top of the rock.
If anyone tried to get at the packet (though who
would ?) the dress would flutter like a signal. She
visualised herself far out. She would leave Chris-

tian and his silly inhibitions and get to that rock.
The roué in green waist belt had smiled at her, their
favourite had deigned yesterday to see that she
was there. She had given a hand up to the tall
adolescent girl, who talked what seemed to her,
might be a Sardinian variant on Italian. She
wasn't going to stay back because of Christian and
his inhibitions of being too thin. She waded out to
tell him.

Christian, naked to the waist, was tea-party
talking to what, at the moment, could not be dis-
tinguished, save as false teeth in a yellow mask.
Shoulders naked as a screen beauty, rose from new
Derry & Toms saxe-blue. Saxe-blue had gone
duck-egg where the sun got it. Those variants of
blue, made Parthenon frieze carving of wet folds
across a torso, no Phidias yet carved. The two
Miss Thistlethwaites bathed twice daily. This one,
the elder, was telling Christian, in a church social
accent, "but you should go to the 'plage' just once
to see it. They dance, they have cocktails, cham-
pagne, everything. They throw money away.
It costs eight francs to get in and then you must pay
for a bathing tent." Christian said the usual right

68

thing, "O" or "no" with inflection and she went on, "and the *waiters* bring out yellow mattresses for you to lie on." Alex knew that Christian had turned his flawless manner on her, like a searchlight. She splashed to let him know she was there. The other Miss Thistlethwaite emerged. Alex saw Chris bow to another set of teeth in another yellow mask, "my sister."

She swam slowly out from them, forgetting.

Forgetting-remembering . . . she remembered Atlantic breakers on miles of virgin sand and sand dunes and behind dunes, American sea-grass. She remembered the European scene, old, old remembrance, steel blue within lotus-blue of lilies. She remembered, as passing from blue-lit to blue-lit window, one places candles on altars, in a cathedral where all is already too-bright. The flame of the sun was so many million candles, burning to its own glory. In it, she was submerged, rising, dropping to straddle the middle of the three land marks. Seated astride, her back to Christian and the Miss Thistlethwaites, she remembered Paestum.

Then she remembered Philae. She could not
remember further.

Her wide eyes stared, hypnotist eyes, past the
final goal, the slippery "last" rock, as she and
Christian called it. Christian, who always pre-
tended not to see her, would tell her, three days
later, just what she had been doing, how at a
given moment, she had risen from sea-water, how
at a given instant, she had sunk back, had turned
her face to the sun, or had parted sea from sea with
arms, so much more adept at this than, he confessed,
he would have credited. Christian would pilot
Christian around his given boulder ; he still took
orders from this Christian. She herself had walked
out of herself, simply kicking garter belt and Deau-
ville sandals to one side and with Deauville sandals
and somewhat weathered satin garter belt, the odd
thing that went with them, trappings, the double
sluice gate that had let her slide past ; the twin
barred double gate was open.

Remembering in that grand sense, she had found,
had nothing to do with those platinum gates of
shining intellect. Mnemoseyne, the Mother of the
Muses . . . was this sort of thing ; remembering.

Christian said the great coral branched cactus trees in the Casino garden were sub-conscious plant life. She had said, "sub-aqueous." The things she thought, were under the water, for all she sat so perched there. Flippantly turning over the pages of the hotel guide book, she had chanced to read to Christian, "Eze. The Phoenicians set up their first temple here, to Isis." Blue. She gathered the blue-impression, like a cloak, about her.

II.

By that the so much happier, by that the so
much wiser, she let impression sway, rather than
jolt, she let voices slip through and past. In the
coral-hued gown that was Christian's favourite,
she let voice mingle, indistinguishable from flutter
of paper vine and rose, the slip-slop of the wine-
waiter and the soft glide of that boy, another
picked "favourite" among the tribe of waiters.
Christian had said, "I think on a whole, I vote for
the bawdy little wine-waiter." Alex said, "the
tall boy—" "the hors-d'œuvres ?" "No," she
said, "the one with those eyes." Then Christian
agreed. "You mean," he said "the one whose
eyes God put in, as the Irish say, with dirty fingers ?'
Yes, God put in his eyes with sooty fingers. The
boy's eye-lashes were smudged in, chimney-sweep
black, about grey-green reedy water.

Inwardly, indistinguishable, by that the so much happier, she knew outwardly her coral gown had given the dame they called the "carnival queen" a jolt. That English lady in the doorway, gathered balance, tried in vain to recapture her usual Duse entrance. Christian muttered over turbot, "now she'll think, after all, you are a smart demi-mondaine." Alex smiled across, into eyes whose usual agate was smoke-blue now, in the new near-bronze. Only now, she realised that he had always outwardly been too white, that she had been inwardly too incandescent. She was cool with flutter of paper vine and roses making tremor in that air, through which passed the bawdy wine-waiter, through which trod Ganymede. She said she would have ice in her white wine, apologetically to Christian, for she knew he thought it was wrong.

A moon, three sizes too large, came up. It could be seen to have come, because of a lane that led from beyond the palm-trees, irrational silver, on off into irrational space. The broad clusters of the date palms hid the moon, that must be three

73

sizes too large to-night, as it had been three sizes
too large last night. The moon seemed not to
have changed, though Christian said, last night, it
looked as if it had fallen off the table. She saw,
then, that the moon was squashed a little sideways,
was still, she persisted, the same size. The moon
was hidden by the date leaves and the swaying
fringe that, this afternoon, she had bent head back
to draw into her perspective. "That powder
tassel," she had said to Christian, "is the date-
blossom." She had not known that. She had
said, "in Egypt—" the unformed sentence was in
its whole implication, a lie. She had not seen date-
palms in blossom in Egypt, neither did Egypt
mean to her what she meant to imply to him, it
did mean. She could not say, she would not say,
blatantly and baldly, "I never so loved Egypt ;
that winter there was not the shock that this is."
She could not say that. He would think it a stilted,
graceless compliment. He would not know that
she loved this frivolous beauty-patch, this corner,
more than she loved Egypt, more than she loved
Greece. She would not let him know how much
she loved it, lest the very mouthing of the words

should let bars down. To speak, requires an intellectual effort. If she spoke, who knows ? Platinum might snap back. If she thought, who knew ?

Platinum had wired in, had set beautifully her impression of the Luxor temple, carved out of mountain, set against blue dome. Too great a beauty for so small a setting, platinum intellect still held it. In a box, in a brain, she held that beauty perfect, her beauty, a lawful heritage. In a box there were a sprinkled smattering of islands, gems, too beautiful but never over-ornate. In the whole box now there was nothing over-ornate. For one moment she would look at those gems, Sorrento, jade-green, Capri, Rhodes, the coast of Cyprus. She would look deep, deep, let hands lift perfection, let fall perfection. She said, "Monte Carlo is a vulgarian's paradise."

Elbows leant on the ledge beside her. They were smooth grey elbows, summer-cut smooth jacket, no dead dining-out black. The coat was the colour of the stone parapet they leant on. For a moment, she dreamt she grew to it, coral against stone ledge. She repeated, "a vulgarian's paradise."

He would not catch the song in her throat. He could not. He could not catch the *c* and the *d* and the minor trembling of a string ; he could not hear the music. She listened to a voice, her own voice, that went on, meticulous in detail, "but the people in the casino are like the things you turn up under an old rug, left all winter in a garden." He would not catch her song, he could not. She said, "you ought just for ten minutes, to go in there, Christian."

A small yacht fluttered pennants, there were arches of tricolour, there were shields, tacked up to lamp-posts. The arc-lights shed incandescence down and into a hollow that was the famous basin of Monte Carlo, into which other yachts rode, fluttering in the over-illumination, gay July 14th streamers and ribbons of the tricolour. Beyond, the Condamine, (rock cut with careless scissors, crudely from black card-board) apparently cast no shadow but served as a double reflector for the moon that now rode high. The moon, she now saw, had been adequately sat on. It was a squashed orange garden cushion, bulged to one side, sat on.

Across the road of the moon, occasional steam launch puffed its little protest, child toy boat into a Japanese lantern strung on a wire across a pond in a birthday-party garden. Behind them, strains of Vienna, from the famous but provincial orchestra, sounded too slowly. She said, "how was I to know that it isn't like—this ?"

He was flicking cigarette ash. He was flicking ash down an area ; a black wedge of dark was the steep drop across a few straggling inadequate peaks of Arizona spike tree. She couldn't think of the name of that tree. It worried her for a moment. For a moment, she wanted bars ever so gently to cast, at least, a shadow. She wanted a shadow of intellect to inform her that she was there. She would fight a little, call up some word to claim her. She had told him about date-palms, she would tell him about this thing. "Did you know this spike tree sort of thing that sticks up all the coast ? " He was looking out, listening to the music. She repeated—"this funny spike thing like burnt matches, stuck up in a child's sand heap is the Arizona—is the Arizona—" but she couldn't get it. He wasn't, anyhow, listening to what she

77

said. He said, "it's actually Strauss they're play-
ing."

She said, though she knew it was Strauss, played
half again too slowly, half-heartedly to shock him,
"it's some sort of Mozart." He said, "it's Strauss—
listen." The place was doing its best to be what
the place always had been. But how was she to
have known (Christian really should have warned
her) that the place was not a bit like what it seemed
to be like, like what she had believed it would be
like, to what presumably it was like ? She said,
"the funniest thing about it is, it's so exactly what
I thought it would be."

Aloe. The word dropped like a pebble into a
pool, set up ripple, recalled more distant ripple.
"Those aloe trees" (he hadn't even noticed) "remind
me of Arizona." They did not. Nothing reminded
her of anything, things served to let slip out, or
served slightly to bar or served to seem to hurry
along, to show the rate at which she moved ; that
simply. *Aloe* did nothing to her. It was a straw
thrown down, that showed simply that she was

moving. The word "aloe" showed that the blue
surface of the water heaved up, sank, but it did
not really matter. The word "aloe" had nothing
to do with that sub-aqueous memory, though the
tree had. Spiked up into midnight blue, the
skeleton shapes stirred, like those Casino garden
cactus branches, other-memory. Christian said,
"what was that blue thing called, under the wall,
where we sat before tea ?"

She had seen him sitting on a wall. But he was
alone then. She had come alone to the café to
meet him, then finding it was too early, had swept
resolutely past the amber-fringed sunshades, to-
ward the Casino steps. She considered it her duty
to go in there. She mustn't go back and not have
been in. Of course, it was easy to see from the
conducted tribe of Americans-off-boats, what it
was like. Provincial. She had formulated in her
mind the term "provincial." What else could it
be ? When she found herself inside, she realized
a dank unearthed element really did exist here.
As she had said to Christian, "it's like the things
you turn up under an old strip of carpet, or a
rotten log, in sunlight." "The abstract idea of the

Casino, at Monte Carlo, was familiar to her from childhood, from meretricious "shockers." But how could she know that the Casino would be as true as that yacht, now anchored in mid-harbour, as that stage-moon, as these trees ? Aloes were painted upright on old-fashioned scenery, yachts lay at painted anchor, the moon moved with mechanical wheeze of rusty wires, the sea heaved like the race-track, in the old stage Ben Hur, the very leaves dropped in the open square, before the Café de Paris, by the exact dozen. Yes, Christian should have warned her. But Christian had said, "it was never really like this, in the season."

Christian asked her now what that flower was. It was a jasmine shaped thing with fern-like, conservatory leaves, a fragile sky-blown thing, another blue. She would always remember that flower, she had no name to give it. "Aloe" dropped unexpectedly into the blue pool of her being, setting up counter ripple. But she knew she had never seen this flower, had no memory-in-forgetting. She had no name to give it. She would remember, always, Christian sitting on a wall between maypole uprights that held shield and clustered French flags. She had seen Christian there, from the Casino window.

She said, "I don't know what that flower is . . . you'd have been amazed. There were six, no, eight croupiers to a table. They were dressed like undertakers. There was one at each end, two in the middle, opposite the spinning wheel, and back of the two, each side in the middle, two separate ones, sitting on the sort of tennis-umpire chairs. They were like dining-room tables with hungry faces, faces just out of an underworld novel. I thought the Casino was a sort of tradition and, like that sort of tradition, just hollow. It wasn't hollow. It was full of maggots. I was there ten minutes."

Christian, only half-aware, listening to the second movement of some pot-pourri of de-jazzed Strauss, said, "you seemed to see a lot in ten minutes."

She said, "you couldn't help it. I just walked past the door-keepers. O yes, first, I had to show them my passport in the outer office. You know I made a mistake. They said, 'what is your profession.' I said 'I am écrivan' (I almost said écrevisse) I almost said, 'I am a crawfish.' They said, 'what do you want here ?' I said, 'I am a writer.

I don't want to play. I only want to watch.'
Now, why did I say that ? They made me wait
twice as long, made out more papers. Now they
have me on their black list. I was there ten mi-
nutes. It was dark, an underworld cellar. A girl
was standing waiting for a table. She loomed out
of cinema smoke, hair shining, cinema face pallid.
There were old, old women, all types. They waited
for the play, then scraped up everything. I don't
know the rules. I don't know how they did it.
But I was sure they just scraped up everything.
There were men crouched down. Where do these
people come from ? There were old, yellow, out-at-
heels Corsican-looking fellows, and old, old ladies.
There were other old ladies who seemed to be sort
of under-studies for those principal old ladies. I
am certain they are were-slugs or something. They
turn, I am certain, into worms and crawl under the
carpet at night. The place was simply crawling."
   Staring into meretricious imitation of stage-
scenery, across the track of an unconvincing slightly
battered stage-moon, just three times as big as life
and twice as natural, she said, "there were gilt
mirrors like a railway station. There were plush

benches—*but* crowded—and a spittoon, filled, with white sawdust (clean enough) at the corner. I got a place perched on the very edge of a plush seat and tried to keep my feet out of the spittoon that was as big—as big as that moon there. When I looked right, left, there were lifted faces looking right, left at me. Are people, then, really desperate? I thought Monte Carlo was a sort of property, a weather-worn property, set up nights when they expected the Lithuania, in at Nice. I thought it was an exploded fallacy like—like—like patriotism, like anything you fancy. I thought it was the American dollar that kept it going, but as old missionary looking dame, who couldn't even find a corner to sit down in, said in a respectable Minneapolis little sad voice, across the dead plush heaviness of the undertaker silence, 'but you know, Katie, you couldn't play even if you *did* want to. There's no room anywhere.' Even if you *did* want to. She obviously did want to. I got up and made room for her by the spittoon. I got over to the window. Just then, the orchestra outside struck up the opening bars of the Marseillaise, as if for my benefit and I began to giggle."

83

"Yes," he said, quite seriously, as if the concert were the only thing that mattered, "that was the beginning. They played their own national hymn first, or something that sounded, as if it couldn't have been anything but it. Anyhow the policemen stood at attention." Christian turned his back to the stage moon. His thin face, in the downpour of electricity, looking like a Basque made-up for a Chelsea Ball. She said, "you ought to paint on a little moustache and wind a handkerchief around your head and be a Spanish gipsy. They all wear fancy-dress here." He did not listen to her. He said, "you see, it *is* Strauss."

She couldn't giggle any more. She could giggle at the Marseillaise, struck up with fantastic aptness, the very second she had reached that window, to view (outside) a painting of some uncatalogued post-Cézanne period. Little spot and dash of colour, no blur, all put on with exact thumb smear, yet all looking almost natural. Her eyes, squinting a little toward that heady sunlight, had perhaps been responsible for its *looking* natural, for it certainly was not. It was the sort of painting you could pull to pieces, grand-stand in the middle, extravagance of bunting, pennants, flags on separate sticks and flags clustered in little .bouquets, yet all somewhat niggling, put in here, there with a fantastic modernistic attempt at pseudo-Victorianism. It was the sort of painting you see across the room at a French impressionistic gallery and wonder how it got there. The sort of thing you pass clustered pears for, and mellow exquisite Cézanne-gardens and bundles of cumulous cherry. It was all wrong certainly. She said, "it was the funniest thing. I waded, simply waded through that room. I had to turn and look once at the ceiling and then a sort of flunkey spied me. The place seemed full of flunkies, apart from the eight undertakers at each table. The minute I bent my head back to look at the ceiling, there was a flunkey saying, 'madame?' with the sort of interrogation that simply shouted 'what are you a mere écrivan or écrevisse lobster doing in here ?' I was a very clean fish. At least, I felt so, not crusted but transparent. He looked right through me. I was the only body in a world of ghosts or the only ghost in a world of bodies. Anyhow, I was different. He said 'madame' with a curling question mark . . . when I stared up at the ceiling. He said 'madame.' "

"What," Chris said, "was there on the ceiling ?"
She said, "clouds. And on the clouds ladies
sitting. The ladies had no clothes on. They were
smoking cigars."

He could not hear the song in her throat. How
could he ? Her little monologue stabbed home.
She liked to torture him with laughing. He was
laughing, as a moth laughs. It was his own des-
cription of his laughter. No one could better it.
He laughed silently, shaking shoulders. He had
said, "I hate moths. I laugh like a moth laughs."
He did not like moths. He loved butterflies,
dragon-flies. He had said, "moths are creepy
things. When I was a small child, one flew in at
our window, in the country, and beat on my face."
A small little boy in a big room had been bruised
by the beat of moth wings ; fantasy, fantastic
imagery. The moth, in its proportion, became a sort
of Arabian Nights roc-moth, a creature of imagin-
ation ; who but Chris had ever said, "I don't like
moths ?" He laughed, as such a moth laughs,
hunching shoulders that would do for wide wings.

86

He had wide wings, little curls at the forehead.
She said, "no. Go to the Chelsea ball as a moth.
Don't paint on a Basque gipsy moustache. Paint
on a moustache on your forehead." He should
paint on a wiry little stick-up sort of feeler thing
or wire it. He should go to a ball as a moth. It
was all fancy dress. "What shall I go as ?"

He could not hear the song in her throat. How
could he ? How could he hear the *e*, the *d*, the *c*
that slid in and the chord that was wrung from
several different bright strings. He could not hear
the song in her throat. "O, Chris, what do you
think," she suddenly remembered, "this morning—
I forgot to tell you." A pebble had been dropped,
"aloe" was a pebble or, appositely, a straw floating.
"Aloe" remembered from nowhere, a word for-
gotten, stirred memory-in-forgetting. The surface of
a pool had been broken, ripple set up ripple. She
said, "Mira-Mare." He said, "what, Alexis ?"
He called her Alexis sometimes, they didn't know
why exactly. "What Alex ?" "You know, I told
you there was a brand-new building, right out of a
band box, at the top of some stairs that I was too
tired to go up ?" "One day—" "Yes, one day,

I told you. It was just after we came. Then this
morning, I saw the place, looking newer than ever
and I climbed up. A sort of janitor person was
there. I told him we'd come back to-morrow
before bathing, about ten—but I don't know."
He listened. She went on, "and what do you think
its name is ? It's called Mira-Mare; Mira, the
Wonderful, and Mare, the Sea, obviously." He
said, "Mira, the Wonderful, Mare, the Sea, obviously.
You go as a seal, to that dance."

III.

Paddy said, the French choose places like this.
Who wouldn't ? She had meant to see Paddy.
There were only seven days ; six and a half, if you
counted the first morning wasted. The first morn-
ing had not been altogether wasted. Christian
said, "do you want to sleep ?" She had said, "no."
She had pulled this strap, that strap, fallen into a
bath, chosen the coolest thing she had. She met
Chris in the hotel lounge, he in his most summer
grey. She wore the flowered chiffon that was,
Chris had said, "autumnal." The chiffon was tea-
colour, blobbed with indefinite rose-pattern. Here,
the tea-coloured rose-pattern did not seem autumnal.
It matched the tobacco under-side of great leaves
that fell one, two, three, slowly so that you could
count them. Before the Café de Paris, they were
swept up ; under the tree at the turn to the sea road,

they lay crumpled ; crushed under her heels, they
gave up scent of summer, were not autumnal.
Christian said that they were not magnolia.

Now the cases were all packed, just the things
for the morning, the coolest she had, her bath
things that would stuff in the top. She had switch-
ed off the middle light ; the bed-lamp, by her side,
cast a superior circle. The overhead lamps were
garish but she hadn't minded. They had blue
shades that served rather to concentrate than to
disperse the overhead crude yellow. The French,
Paddy said, swarmed down here from Brittany.
All those sensitive blue eyes in pale yet weathered
faces, she judged, were Bretons. Paddy had told
her in London, there were many French here.
Monte Carlo.

She might have gone to see Patricia, but why ?
Paddy had an apartment in the rue or boulevard
de something. She rented it in the season, lived
here in the summer to economize, but Alex couldn't
find it. She didn't try, superlatively hard, to
find it. She had seen Paddy, in one of the fiacres,
with the cream-coloured awning and the tassels,
sunburnt, with teeth. Paddy was wearing a sort

of chintz hat, was chattering to a friend, probably hadn't seen her. What could she say anyhow, to Paddy, to excuse her casualness ? What could she say to Paddy ? Later she might say, "I have taken an apartment." She might say, "we have taken an apartment, come to see us."

Mira-Mare. She said Mira-Mare. It was a charm. It held her up, supported her, so that she could sit erect, her feet stretched sideways, out from the bed, wrapped round in the cool sheet. She wanted to see Christian, just to say good-night. She had said, "if the door's open, just pop in to let me know, you are back." At the hotel door, downstairs, she had insisted, "it's only ten. I must pack anyway. Do your duty by the town, as I did this afternoon with the casino ; go see something, maybe that outdoor movie." He had held the bamboo and bead curtain for her, waited. "O do go, do go, Christian. Someone must see the fireworks. If I pack to-night, I am quite free to-morrow." There had been occasional mild explosions and flickering of blue light. But now the show, whatever it was, was over. The traffic, last night, had made her think of the "battle of the taxis." Last night, she lay thinking, listening to the hoot, the steady rumble, like Piccadilly traffic. The 14th of July, of course, every one would be out. Last night she had been frightened, said, "Italy, France." She was swept into a circle of terror, "France, Italy." She loved France— Italy and Monaco, a beauty patch, to be swept under. No, no, no her heart protested. Now there was shrill continual trembling, like (Christian said) "wind in telegraph wires." They were, she was certain, tree-toads ; he called them courtillières. He said, "in the Cevannes, they called them courtillières." She said, "I'm sure they're tree-toads." The shrill persistent song of the far insects thrilled in her, like her own blood. The cry beat in her, was her. She was beating with it, was it, wrapped in the cool sheet.

A clock far, far, far, far, struck one. It dropped *one* into a pool of being. Her feet, stark straight across the narrow bed, stuck out in the mummy wrappings of the cool sheet. *One.* Far, far, far *one* sounded. It fell like a meteor. *One* came from another world, the human element was alien. She had been numbed, hypnotised by the high wind in telegraph wires of the courtillières, that Chris said were not tree-toads. Spiked sound, spiked up, defined yet motivated, like sea-tentacles under water. The wind in telegraph wires of the courtillières were spikey, yet moved in the fragrance of that element. The fragrance of the new-found element, in which their wings moved like antennae under water, was more familiar to her than this bell sound. *One* dropped like a meteor, from another planet.

One broke the charm, yet still was part of that charm. *One* recalled space, time, broke like a careless hand through paper scenery. *One* swept away the mythopoeic sense of her, pulled it aside like cheap mosquito netting. *One*, sounding, sounded across (now she noticed) belated trail of feet, a group, whose whispered Italian made a Longhi of the street, outside the window. Yesterday, leaning out, she had said to Christian, "it's not a street, it's not an alley, it's a calle." Longhi was outside and moonlight, the courtillières were a mosquito netting, sound and shape were punctured, *here* and

there, separated by that gauze curtain. *One* was
a hand lifted to drop, raised to lift that curtain.
Feet shuffled. All the motor cars, in all the world,
had passed here last night. Last night, there was
a trail, like the battle of the taxis.

The shrill-shrill-shrill (wind in telegraph wires)
of the courtillières had set her heart beating else-
where. Her mythopoeic heart, that she had
almost forgotten, had struck like a gong within her.
Even that first morning, as she had dragged out her
silliest things to belie it, it chattered in and against
that gong. She had chattered interminably about
the few belated hotel diners and mouthed epigrams
across at Christian, at the expense of the Americans-
off-boats who trailed in, never less than fifty. She
had decided at dinner, that the French pseudo-
child, with the chiffon train and long bob brushing
glaringly unburnt, immature bare shoulders was
sheer Pinero 1930 and that it was she who had
attuned sensitive ears to catch the very intonation
of the colonel as, three tables down, he told the
Carnival Queen's first understudy, about Percy. It

94

was she who had repeated all the Percy jargon, so that now, already in two days, Percy was a feature in their lives, an entity as precise, as embodied as the boy with the soot-lashes or their glorified favourite perched, with or without "winged sandals," in platinum grey waist band, on the "last" rock. It was she who had discovered, if you take five Italian words and pronounce them French, you are talking Monagesque ; a new language.

In less than a week, their lives had shaped to two lives, their separate abstract mythopoeic life and the personal concrete hotel life. In the almost empty dining room, there was flutter of paper vines and paper roses, the steady subdued buzz of electric fans and the shuffle of waiters, or the dining-room was crowded suddenly with never less than fifty Americans-off-boats, who seemed to be stuffed, cheap cotton imitations, into their perfect doll-house. Their house was empty ; long glacial hall-ways were cool with slats of closed shutters, to strike off radiant gold bars. The rooms, for the most part, were empty, half shuttered, with wide doors. The servants, sitting chattering in empty rooms, rose, half guilty, as they passed, down the interminable hallway. It was a large doll-house with tiny rooms, half empty, then stuffed with crude imitation toy-dolls, spilled out, by the cheap gross. "Of course," she said to Christian, unexpectedly on the defensive, "you can't judge Americans by these, any more than you could English people, if Liverpool and Manchester *travelled*." A little barb stung out, as she bent to peel her ripe fig and Christian answered, "true. But there aren't so many of them. Manchester and Liverpool might travel, by the handful, but never by the million." It was the boy across, upset him. "Why," he had asked Alex, "do American boys always look fat and milk-fed ?" She had flared (why ?), "they don't, Christian. If Liverpool and Manchester travelled" et cetera.

Such were the empty straws flung down to show the heaving of the wave beneath them.

Such and such an empty straw, they flung down to show the heaving of the wave beneath them. Percy would do for a long time. If they stayed here a month, Percy would do all that time. Percy would come up, he was a new language. "Now," said the Colonel, "it's this way, I say 'Percy do not,'

I shake a finger at him I say, 'no, no.' Percy felt
in my pockets for the cigars. I said 'no, no.'"
The carnival queen (it was the real one that time)
said without enthusiasm, "yes they *are* so uncanny,"
but Percy's father, the colonel, went on (he must
have felt the sympathy in Alex's chiffon back),
"I said 'no, no' but Percy said 'urrugh—urrugh—
r'm, r'm, r'm, uurgh.' But I said, 'you can't Percy,
you've had one to-day already,' but Percy just
insisted 'r'm, r'm, r'm, ooorgh.'" The language
of Percy was now a common inheritance, they
jabbered it when they saw the Colonel or any sort
of Colonel, in the distance. But they had yet to
make out what Percy was doing that day when the
colonel was heard, across finger bowls and peaches,
"and then Percy jumped *right* into the polar bear's
cave."

Bright flame shot up, slashed hole in casual
memory. They had watched a forest fire on the
hills, the flame against evening, fluttered like yellow
cheese-cloth. Then flame wavered, fragile as paper,
straight upward, incense. There was heady visual
memory of clustered rock and unexplored cove and
a garden that was built out on a separate island

with a thin breakwater of native stone to join it. There was a villa, whose roof was one gigantic sundial, there was a villa whose pots were enamelled bright blue and bunches of cultivated thistles oddly fumed lavender thistle smoke up into a sky that was almost white from shining radiance. There were the awnings, Chris called, "snails," and that one house, built blank square with just one huge green snail awning, clinging to its sunside. There were the outsides of villas whose insides could be exactly gauged by their exquisite proportion and there were the smouldering terra-cotta villas whose taste was so atrocious that Christian called them "restful." "I would like," he said, "to have one of the worst of those Moorish villas and one cactus in the front yard." There were steps that led skyward that were hardly distinguishable from irregular aged walls, except that there were no iron-red spikes of wild vervain, growing from the graduated irregularity of their stones. There were the inevitable geraniums, only a little burnt about the bases, and the terracotta was shown to be as cool as glazed bath-room tiles by the rabid gash of hollyhock shaped hybiscus to show what red could be. There were cool immaculate clusters of single white oleander, as delicate as orange blossom and the willow-like branches of other oleander that was now over. There were the turned-up hummocks of raw earth, in the Casino garden, that Chris said were one bank of lilies in the spring and over and through it all like darts puncturing a clear canvas (those darts of ecstasy to ruin a still picture) were the shrill whirl and whirl and sweep and swoop of swallows. There were swallows to shrill continually, early morning, late evening before the tireless monotonous drone of those musical wind-swept telegraph wires (courtillières) dragged one to sea-bottom. There were swallows to drag one out of sleep, tireless dart on dart, blue-blue to show blue, what blue should be.

"O hello, sleeping ?" "No, I've been sitting here. Don't switch on that light. I turned the little one off, just as it struck one. Here—wait—I'll find it." He had pushed back the screen, then, carefully replaced it. He stood for one moment in the terrific glare of the blue bulbs of the ceiling lights, which he immediately switched off. The meretricious, subtle little bed-light threw its little circle on the floor, on the sheet. He came toward her, his face bent toward her, she clutched the smooth stuff of his summer grey cloth, he sat down, he said, "I did go to the out-of-doors movie. It was a scream." She said, "what was it?" He said, "why something so old as the hills that even I had never heard of it. French." "Funny?" "In that way, yes. It was really rather queer, the moon was and that sheet of light across heads in a garden and a fountain, off stage, somewhere. They took up too much time in the interval, with a sort of patriotic concert and some speeches. That's why I'm so late."

She let her fingers go. She had been waiting for this but she could never tell him. Her fingers, clutching the smooth cloth to which, this evening she had wanted to grow, coral to grey rock, would belie the thing within her. Within her, was the steady flame that swept up like that forest fire, but subtleized, spread out, flung out, and over and under, so that she was no more participant of that flame than the fragrance of the flower is of its heady summer-pollen. She was the fragrance of the

flower, the quivering in the air that set those wire
things ringing, she was the shrill upward sweep of
blue that spoiled a quiet canvas and she was the
picture, created in her mind, as well as the outer
picture. There were tags for this, Tao, Greek,
Egyptian. She had no finger to put on that tag.
There was a tag. "Do you remember once you
turned out my pocket-book, in the car going to—
to Sion—and I said, 'there's nothing but some bills'
and you read something I had scratched down on an
old envelope ?" His hand had closed over the
hand that she had let drop. His shoulder, moving
a little, hunching or shaking a little, was the sort
of odd way he had of loving, no more than a wing
moving. The touch of that exaggerated shoulder
against her sleeping jacket, was the bone and sinew
of a wing, was the raw structure of a thing that was
moving, whirling, that was spread out to spoil the
world about her. The raw bone was the merest
skeleton, their love was the merest frame-work.
He said, (he never listened to what she said), "I
saw Percy's father and the duchess and the other
marchese and those two boys." She said, as if this
was all that there ever was between them, "did the

smaller one still wear his bandages for sun-burn ?"
and half remembered that tag, *the moth having seen
the light* . . . "I remember that tag."

Words, repetitions, framing of words means bars
down. The bars would fall, there would be swoop
of dangerous thought, to pass dangerously, like the
train, before their bathing beach, which she had
not yet seen pass. "Is there time to bathe to-
morrow ?" He said, "why not ?" She said,
"almost the loveliest tree (or should I say the
maddest ?) is that one just as you cross the track,
that looks sort of—sort of crippled and has that
blue flame about it." He said, "I don't yet think
those blue things are morning-glories." She said,
"which is your favourite tree ?" He said, "I think
I like that one cactus that grows at the Casino gate.
The one with the triangular rosettes that might
be fresh buds." She said, "sub-conscious." "Sub-
aqueous," he said, remembering her word. She
said, "you remember that bit of paper, in my
pocket-book, with the Tao tag (I remember it now)
you turned out, on the way to Sion ? *The moth
having seen the light*—" He said, *"never returns
to the darkness."*